A Note *from Michelle about*
THE PROBLEM WITH PEN PALS

Hi! I'm Michelle Tanner. I'm nine years old. And I have an on-line pen pal who's way cooler than I am. That's why I told her I was the host of a new kid's program on TV. But I'm not. And now she wants me to send her a videotape of the show!

My best friends, Cassie and Mandy, are going to help me make one. But we have to keep it a secret from my family. And that's going to be tough. My family is huge!

There's my dad and my two older sisters, D.J. and Stephanie. But that's not all.

My mom died when I was little. So my uncle Jesse moved in to help Dad take care of us. So did Joey Gladstone. He's my dad's friend from college. It's almost like having three dads. But that's still not all!

First Uncle Jesse got married to Becky Donaldson. Then they had twin boys, Nicky and Alex. The twins are four years old now. And they're so cute.

That's nine people. Our dog, Comet, makes ten. Sure, it gets kind of crazy sometimes. But I wouldn't change it for anything. It's so much fun living in a full house!

FULL HOUSE™ MICHELLE novels

Available from MINSTREL Books

FULL HOUSE™
Michelle

The Problem with Pen Pals

Maggie McMahon

A Parachute Book

A MINSTREL® BOOK

Published by POCKET BOOKS
New York   London   Toronto   Sydney   Tokyo   Singapore

A MINSTREL PAPERBACK *Original*

A Minstrel Book published by
POCKET BOOKS, a division of Simon & Schuster Inc.
1230 Avenue of the Americas, New York, NY 10020

A PARACHUTE BOOK

READING Copyright © and ™ 1998 by Warner Bros.

FULL HOUSE, characters, names and all related indicia are trademarks of Warner Bros. © 1998.

ISBN: 0-671-01732-2

First Minstrel Books printing October 1998

10 9 8 7 6 5 4 3 2 1

A MINSTREL BOOK and colophon are registered trademarks of Simon & Schuster Inc.

Cover photo by Schultz Photography

Printed in the U.S.A.

The Problem with
Pen Pals

Chapter

1

♥ "I can't wait!" nine-year-old Michelle Tanner whispered to her best friend, Cassie Wilkins. "I hope my pen pal is from a really cool place. Like Alaska or France or China!"

"Me, too," Cassie whispered back.

Michelle had been dreaming about her pen pal all last week. Now it was finally Thursday. The big day at school—the day she would get an E-Kids pen pal.

E-Kids was a pen pal group made up

of students from all over the world. The *E* stood for *electronic*.

E-Kids didn't just write to their pen pals on paper. They wrote to them on-line—on a computer. Using E-mail!

"I hope my pen pal likes the same things I do," Mandy Metz said. Mandy was Michelle's other best friend.

"That's why we filled out those forms," Michelle reminded her. "So E-Kids could find us our perfect match."

Last week all the kids in Michelle's class filled out a special paper. It asked questions like what were their favorite colors, favorite hobbies, favorite subject in school. Stuff like that. The E-Kids computer used the answers to make perfect pen-pal matchups.

"Jeff Farrington," Mrs. Yoshida called from her desk. "Come up and get your pen pal."

2

Jeff ran up to the front of the class. Mrs. Yoshida handed him a piece of paper.

"No way!" Jeff clapped a hand to his face as he looked at the paper. "Mrs. Y, this says *you're* my pen pal!"

The class burst out laughing. Jeff liked to make jokes.

"Mandy Metz!" Mrs. Yoshida called out.

Mandy hurried to the front of the room. She raced back to her seat, grinning at her piece of paper.

"My pen pal lives in Mexico!" Mandy exclaimed. "And she takes ballet lessons. She loves volleyball. And her favorite subject is math. Just like me!"

"That's great," Michelle said. Mandy was so lucky. She and her pen pal had a lot in common.

While Mrs. Yoshida called out some

more names, Michelle daydreamed about her pen pal. *I hope she likes soft-ball and pets and science—just like me!*

"Okay. That's it." Mrs. Yoshida broke through Michelle's thoughts. "Now everyone has a pen pal."

"Huh?" Michelle raised her hand. "What about me?" she asked her teacher. "I didn't get a pen pal."

Mrs. Yoshida searched through the papers on her desk. "That's odd. There must have been some kind of mix-up."

"E-Kids probably couldn't find anyone who'd want to write to you, Michelle," Jeff called out. "You're too weird!"

A few kids giggled.

Michelle smiled at Jeff. "That can't be true. They found *you* a pen pal, didn't they?"

"That's enough, you two," Mrs. Yoshida said. Then she turned to Michelle. "I'm sure we can straighten this out, Michelle. Hang in there until tomorrow. We'll find you a great pen pal."

"Okay." Michelle sighed. She felt terrible. She was the only one in her whole class who didn't have a pen pal!

Mandy and Cassie made plans to stay late after school. They wanted to go online at the computer lab next to their classroom. Michelle had to go home alone.

She plodded up to her front door and pushed it open. Her dog, Comet, leaped up and licked her face. His tail pounded the floor.

"Not now, Comet," Michelle said, patting his soft golden fur. "I don't feel like playing."

"Hola!" Michelle heard someone say. She looked up. Her father stood next to the couch. He was wearing a big Mexican sombrero on his head and was holding a spoon.

"Hola!" Danny said again. "That means *hello* in Spanish. Are you ready for taco night?"

Michelle's dad was always trying out different recipes. He had a special apron for every season and holiday. Sometimes he even dressed up for his special dinners.

"Sure, Dad," Michelle mumbled.

"Good," Danny said. "Why don't you go set the table now, so you won't have to do it later."

"But, Dad," Michelle complained. "I hate setting the table. Do I have to?"

Danny nodded. "It's your turn. Next week D.J. has to do it."

Michelle dropped her books by the steps and went to the kitchen to get the

6

dishes. She set places for all nine people in her family. We're going to need lots of tacos, Michelle thought. There are a *ton* of people to feed.

Besides Michelle and her dad, there were her older sisters, Stephanie and D.J. Then there was her dad's best friend, Joey Gladstone. After Michelle's mom died, Joey moved into the basement apartment to help out. That made five people. Uncle Jessie and Aunt Becky stayed on the third floor with their four-year-old twins, Nicky and Alex. That made a total of nine people living in their house.

Usually Michelle's family cheered her up, but right now Michelle didn't think anyone could.

Michelle picked up her books and dragged herself upstairs to the bedroom she shared with Stephanie. Stephanie was thirteen and in the eighth grade. She was sprawled across the bed on her side of the room, reading a fashion magazine.

Michelle sighed as she sprinkled some food into the bowl in her fuzzy black guinea pig's cage.

"What's wrong?" Stephanie asked, glancing up from her magazine.

"I had the worst day," Michelle said. She explained to Stephanie what happened in school. That she didn't get an E-Kids pen pal. And that Jeff Farrington had said it was because she was weird.

"Don't worry about what Jeff said. You're not *that* weird!" Stephanie joked. "And you'll have a pen pal tomorrow," she said. "So it's no big deal, right?" She went back to reading her magazine.

Michelle stared at her sister. It *was*

a big deal! Michelle was left out of all the fun today. And she was the only one!

Then Michelle had a horrible thought. What if she *never* got a pen pal? What if Jeff were right? What if E-Kids really *couldn't* find anyone who wanted to write to her?

Chapter
2

❤ "Hey, Michelle!" Mandy and Cassie yelled. "Over here!"

"Hi, guys!" Michelle hurried to sit with her friends. They had saved her a seat on the school bus.

"Guess what?" Cassie said. "I got an E-mail from my pen pal, Hilary, at home this morning! Her cat, Missy, had kittens. It was so cool to hear from her."

"My pen pal, Marisol, promised to E-mail me at school today," Mandy said. "She's going to teach me a few Spanish words."

"E-Kids is the best thing ever," Cassie declared. Then she looked at Michelle. "Oops! I forgot that you don't have a pen pal yet."

"Sorry," Mandy added. "I forgot, too."

Michelle yawned. "It's okay," she said. Then she yawned again.

"Why are you so tired, Michelle?" Mandy asked.

Michelle rubbed her eyes. "Because I had an awful dream last night," she answered. "Then I couldn't go back to sleep. It was super scary!"

"What happened?" Cassie asked.

"I dreamed that I never got a pen pal. And that I had to write letters to myself!"

Jeff turned around and leaned over the back of his seat. "At least you'd always know your pen pal's address!" he joked.

Michelle tried not to laugh, but she couldn't help it. She and her friends giggled until they reached school. But by the time they got to Mrs. Yoshida's classroom, Michelle was worried. She hoped that her dream from the night before wouldn't come true.

Michelle was still worrying when she sat down at her desk. She reached into her pocket for a quarter. Heads, she would get a pen pal. Tails, she wouldn't.

She flipped the coin in the air and caught it. Then she peeked into her hand.

Tails. No pen pal. This was the worst!

Mrs. Yoshida hurried down the aisle. She stopped next to Michelle's desk and smiled. Then she handed her a piece of paper. "Here it is, Michelle," the teacher said. "Your pen pal's name and on-line address."

"Yes!" Michelle cried in relief. "Thanks, Mrs. Yoshida," she said, and looked at the paper. Her pen pal's name was Janie. I can't wait to write to her! Michelle thought.

Mrs. Yoshida handed out charts to the whole class. They listed the times when kids could go on-line with pen pals who lived in other countries.

"You'll each have a chance to go to the school computer lab every day," Mrs. Yoshida said. "Michelle, you can be the first to go this morning. E-Kids arranged for you and your pen pal to be on-line at the same time."

"All right!" Michelle cried. She rushed next door to the lab. A teacher showed her how to use the computer. Soon Michelle was writing her very first E-mail letter:

Dear Janie,

Hi, I'm Michelle Tanner, your new pen pal!

I'm nine years old, and in the fourth grade.

I have a huge family. Also a dog, and a fluffy black guinea pig. I love softball and butter crunch ice cream.

My favorite colors are pink and blue. Please tell me everything about you!

Your pen pal,
Michelle

Michelle hit the send key. In a minute Janie wrote back!

Hi, Michelle,

I don't know how E-Kids matched you and me.

We're total opposites!

I *don't* have a big family. I *hate* all sports.

I even hate butter crunch ice cream.

I don't have any pets, because all animals *STINK!*

And I think the color pink is dumb!

Don't bother writing again. I'm finding another pen pal.

Janie

Michelle stared at the letter on the computer screen in disbelief. Could this really be happening to her?

Chapter

3

♥ Michelle felt awful as she walked with Mrs. Yoshida to the teachers' lounge at lunchtime. She felt awful as Mrs. Yoshida dialed E-Kids. She felt awful as her teacher talked on the phone.

It's not fair, Michelle thought. She lowered her head. Janie didn't even give me a chance. Now I'll never have a pen pal. They'll never find a match for me.

Mrs. Yoshida wrote something on a piece of paper. She hung up the phone and turned to smile at Michelle.

"I've got great news!" Mrs. Yoshida exclaimed. "Your new pen pal sounds like fun. Her name is Darla, and she lives in England."

"England? That's kind of cool," Michelle said.

"You can go back to the computer lab and write to Darla after you finish lunch," Mrs. Yoshida said. "She won't be able to answer right away. But E-Kids said her letter will be on the computer after the weekend—first thing Monday."

Michelle gave her teacher a big hug. "Thanks, Mrs. Yoshida."

In the lunchroom, Michelle gobbled down her peanut butter and banana sandwich. Then she hurried back to the computer lab to write to Darla:

Dear Darla,

I can't wait to hear from you! It must be so cool to live in England!

I'm nine years old and in the fourth grade. I live in San Francisco, in a big old house. There are nine people in my family, including me!

I have two older sisters. Then there's my dad's best friend, and my aunt and uncle, and their twin boys. My dad is the host of a TV show. It's called *Wake Up, San Francisco.*

I love softball. And art. And my favorite colors are pink and blue.

What about you? What do you like? Hurry up and write back!

Michelle

Michelle clicked the send button.

There, she thought. Darla knows all about me. Now I just have to wait until Monday. Then I'll see if Darla wants to be my pen pal—or not.

"Wait up, Michelle!" Cassie called on Monday morning. She and Mandy leaped off the bus and rushed to catch up to Michelle. "Where are you going in such a hurry?"

"To the computer lab," Michelle replied. "I want to be there the minute it opens."

"I guess you want to see if Darla wrote back," Cassie said.

"I bet she did," Mandy added. "I bet she really wants to be your pen pal."

"I hope so," Michelle said. She still felt awful that Janie had dumped her. Would Darla do the same thing?

Mandy and Cassie followed Michelle

into the computer lab. Michelle sat down at a computer and opened her E-mail box. Seconds later a message appeared on the screen:

Dear Michelle,

It's so great to meet you! Your family sounds really fun. I'm an only child. So, I think you're lucky to have so many people in your house!

I am also nine years old and in grade four. And I love softball and art, just like you! And guess what my favorite colors are? Pink and blue!

I'm also a model for Action Jeans. Maybe you've heard of them? Write back soon!

Darla

"Darla sounds great!" Michelle exclaimed. "And I think she really likes me!"

"I can't believe your pen pal is a

model!" Cassie's eyes opened wide. "That is so cool!"

"I'm writing back to Darla right now," Michelle said.

Dear Darla,
    Wow! We like all the same stuff! Please send me a photo of yourself—in your Action Jeans!
    I'll send you a picture of me, too. I wonder if we look alike?
                                    Michelle

"I guess you found the perfect pen pal," Mandy said, staring at the computer screen.

"That is so cool," Cassie said again. "Now we're all happy!"

"Yay!" Michelle said. "Totally happy!"

"You should send Darla your E-mail address for your home computer,"

Mandy told her. "That way you can talk even when you're not in school."

"Good idea," Michelle said. She added the address to her letter and hit the send key.

Then she beamed at Cassie and Mandy. "I think having a pen pal is going to be the best thing that ever happened to me!"

Chapter

4

♥ "Michelle, what are you doing?" Stephanie gazed around the living room with a frown. "You're making a mess in here. Dad's going to have a fit. You know how neat he likes things."

Michelle pulled another photo album off the shelf. Other albums lay scattered on the floor. Boxes filled with more photos were stacked on the coffee table.

"I'm supposed to send Darla a picture of me," Michelle explained. "But it can't be just *any* photo. I mean, Darla is a model. So, I need a really *cool* one."

Stephanie picked up Michelle's fourth-grade school picture from a shelf. "This one is really cute." She showed it to Michelle. "Send her this."

Michelle gazed at the picture and shook her head. "That one won't impress Darla," Michelle told her.

"You don't have to impress your friends," Stephanie said. "Darla will like you just the way you are."

"But I want Darla to think I'm special. Like she is," Michelle replied.

"Michelle—" Stephanie began.

"This is it!" Michelle interrupted. She picked up a photograph of her whole family.

It was a great picture. Nicky and Alex were trying to climb onto Comet's back. Michelle, Stephanie, and D.J. were tugging on Comet's leash. They were trying to keep him from running away. Aunt Becky and Uncle Jesse were cracking up. Danny and Joey were trying to look serious.

"What is it?" Stephanie asked.

"This—it's perfect," Michelle said, holding up the photograph. "Darla thinks having a big family is really great," she explained. "So I can send her this picture. That should totally impress her."

Stephanie shook her head. "You don't get it," she said. "You should just be yourself, Michelle."

"Right," Michelle said. "Now I need to find something else to send Darla. Something extra, extra cool."

"I give up!" Stephanie said, and bounded up the stairs.

Michelle searched the living room. She

needed her brand-new glow-in-the-dark paints. She had planned to save the paints to make a special picture for D.J.'s birthday.

Darla would really like these, Michelle thought. I can always give D.J. something else.

Michelle found a small box and tucked the paints inside with the picture of Michelle and her family. Darla's going to be really surprised, Michelle thought as she wrote her pen pal a note:

Dear Darla,
　　I'm so glad that E-Kids matched us up! I hope you like the picture and the paints.
　　E-mail me soon!

Your pen pal,
Michelle

The next morning Michelle raced to

the computer lab. She couldn't wait to see if she had a letter from Darla.

Michelle opened her E-mail box. The words NO NEW MESSAGES popped onto the screen.

Michelle frowned. Did Darla hate her surprise? Michelle wondered. Then she remembered that her father had just mailed the gift to England the day before.

Duh! Michelle smacked herself on the forehead. Darla didn't even get the package yet! I'll just have to be patient.

There was no E-mail from Darla on the school computer the next day. Or the day after that. Or the day after that. And nothing at home either.

Michelle ordered herself to be patient. Getting mail to England must take longer than she thought.

About two weeks later, Michelle sat at

the computer in her father's study. Why haven't I heard from Darla? she wondered. It's been more than two weeks since I mailed that package. She was about to turn on the computer, when she heard the doorbell ring.

"Michelle!" Aunt Becky called from downstairs. "You have a package—from England!"

Chapter
5

♥ "A package from England!" Michelle ran to the front door.

A delivery man waited next to Aunt Becky. He held a large envelope under one arm. "Are you Michelle Tanner?" he asked.

"Yes, I am," Michelle replied, a big grin spreading across her face.

"Sign here, please." The man handed Michelle a slip of paper and a pen.

Michelle had never signed for a package before. She carefully wrote her name. She dotted the *i* in *Michelle* with a tiny heart.

The man handed her the envelope.

Michelle glanced at the name and address written across the label. "Darla Brown," she read. "I wonder what it could be?"

Michelle followed Aunt Becky into the living room and plopped herself down on the couch. Then she tore the envelope open and peeked inside.

"Wow! It's an ad for Action Jeans!" She showed Aunt Becky a page carefully cut out of a magazine.

In the picture a pretty girl with brown hair and brown eyes leaned against a tree. She wore wide-bottom jeans with a striped T-shirt. She had a friendly grin and a sprinkling of freckles across her nose.

"This is Darla!" Michelle exclaimed. "She looks really nice."

Michelle caught sight of something sparkly at the bottom of the envelope. She reached in and pulled out two handfuls of glitter stickers.

"Look what else Darla sent me!" Michelle exclaimed. "Stars! She is so cool!"

"I'd say you have a fantastic pen pal," Aunt Becky told her.

"The best," Michelle answered. "I'm going to write her a thank-you letter right now. I mean, a thank-you *E-mail!*"

Michelle raced upstairs to her dad's study. She flipped on the computer and clicked onto her E-mail box.

YOU'VE GOT MAIL! the computer announced.

A letter from Darla popped onto the screen:

Dear Michelle,

Thanks so much for the special paints and card. Also for the funny picture. You and your family look really nice. And friendly!

Sorry I didn't write sooner. I was very busy with modeling. I'm flying to Paris this weekend. It should be lots of fun!

How is everything with you?
Write back soon!

Your pen pal,
Darla

Awesome, Michelle thought.

She clicked SAVE to keep Darla's letter. She printed a copy, too. Then she clicked on ANSWER MAIL.

She wrote back to Darla:

Dear Darla,

Thanks for the special delivery!

You look so pretty in the Action Jeans ad. And the stickers are terrific. I'm going to put them all over my backpack!

Not much is happening with me. We lost our softball game the other day. Boo!

After the game I went bike riding with my two best friends, Cassie and Mandy.

Write back soon. And have fun in Paris!

Michelle

Michelle showed Darla's letter to Aunt Becky and the twins. She showed it to D.J., Joey, her dad, and Uncle Jesse. They all thought it was exciting, too.

"Wow," Jesse said. "I can't believe Darla travels to places like Paris. That's incredible."

* * *

Stephanie flew into the kitchen. "Sorry I'm late," she called. "What's that?" She nodded at Darla's letter. Michelle let her read it.

"Darla has a really amazing life," Stephanie said. She handed the paper back to Michelle.

Darla's life *was* amazing, Michelle thought. She was a model. She got to travel all over the world and wear pretty clothes.

Michelle frowned. Why did I have to write to Darla about my dumb softball game? she wondered. And models probably don't care about riding bikes, either!

Suddenly Michelle felt really, really boring.

"Did Becky tell you all our big news?" Danny said at dinner that night.

"You mean about the new part of our

34

show we're doing on *Wake Up, San Francisco?"* Becky asked. She shook her head. "I didn't tell them yet."

"Something new?" Joey's eyes gleamed. He smoothed back his hair. "If you need a new star, I'm available."

Becky laughed. "Sorry, buddy, but I think you're a little too old. It's for kids, with kid stars."

"But I look young for my age," Joey said.

Jesse laughed. "You mean you *act* young for your age."

"Joey, I guess you could come to the auditions tomorrow." Danny grinned. "But I think we need a *real* kid to host the 'Frisco Kids' spot."

"Wait a minute," Stephanie said. "Exactly what is 'Frisco Kids'?"

"It's a short report for kids," Becky explained. "We want to try having two junior hosts. They'll talk about what young people are doing all over the city."

Michelle caught her breath. She had a great idea! If Darla could be a model, maybe Michelle could be a TV star!

"Dad, can I be a junior host for the show?" she asked.

"Well . . ." Danny said. "You'll have to try out just like everybody else."

"That's okay," Michelle answered. "I don't want any special help. Please, Dad, can I?"

Danny nodded. "Sure!"

"All right!" Michelle cheered.

"Break a leg, Michelle," Joey said.

"Break a leg?" Michelle repeated. "That's not very nice!"

"Don't worry," Aunt Becky told her. "That means good luck in show business."

"Then I hope Michelle breaks *two* legs!" Nicky cried.

Everyone laughed.

Michelle smiled to herself as she sipped her milk. Now I *really* have something cool to tell Darla!

Chapter
6

Hi, Darla!

Are you there? I have some really exciting news to tell you. I'm going to be the junior host of "Frisco Kids." It's part of my dad's TV show. I'll get to report on all the fun stuff kids do in San Francisco! Isn't it great?

Michelle

♥ Michelle and Darla had set up a special computer date that morning so they could E-mail back and forth at the same time. It was the start of the school day for Michelle. And almost dinner-time for Darla in England.

Michelle pressed the send key. She glanced at Cassie and Mandy typing to their pen pals. Then Darla's answer appeared on the computer screen:

Hi, Michelle!
That sounds so cool! Will you please, please send me a video of your show?
I have some great news, too! I'm going to be the model for Pretty Petals perfume! We start taking pictures next week. At Buckingham Palace—where the Queen of England lives!

Michelle gasped as she read Darla's letter. She quickly typed her reply:

Dear Darla,
Sure, I'll send you a tape. I can't be-

lieve you're going to meet the queen! Wow! And I love Pretty Petals perfume. My dad gave me some for my ninth birthday. I wonder if you'll get tons of perfume for free. I know you'll get to wear some really cool clothes in the ads. Maybe even an outfit from Paris! How was Paris, anyway?

Michelle waited only a minute before Darla wrote back:

Dear Michelle,
I climbed to the top of the Eiffel Tower. And I bought a whole packet of postcards to send you. But the wind blew them out of my hands! They must have landed on top of somebody's head! Ha-ha!

Michelle read Darla's letter and laughed.

"Time to say good-bye to your pen

pals." Mrs. Yoshida poked her head into the computer room.

Michelle typed:

Darla,
  Got to go! Bye!

Darla typed back:

Michelle,
  Don't forget to send me your video!
Good luck with your new TV show!

Darla signed off. Michelle stared at the computer screen. She read Darla's last message again.

Why did I do that? Michelle thought. I was supposed to tell Darla about the "Frisco Kids" tryouts. Now Darla thinks that I'm *already* a junior host.

And how am I going to send Darla a

tape of the show when the auditions haven't even started yet?

At least my audition is today, Michelle thought. But then she thought of something else—something really terrible. What if I don't get the part?

Chapter 7

♥ *Bonk!*

Michelle bounced a ball onto the pavement. She and Mandy and Cassie were playing four-square at recess.

Michelle aimed the ball at a cement square drawn in blue chalk on the ground. The ball missed the square. It bounced up and hit Cassie's left shoulder.

"Ouch! Michelle, that's the second time you missed!" Cassie yelled.

"You're not paying attention," Mandy said.

"I guess not. Sorry." Michelle sighed. "I have to talk to you guys. I have a problem."

"What's the matter?" Mandy asked.

"Well, I . . . um . . . I kind of told Darla that I'm the junior host of 'Frisco Kids,' " Michelle replied.

"What?" Cassie asked. "Why did you do that?"

"I didn't really mean to," Michelle began. "But it . . . it just happened."

"Being the host of a TV show *would* be cool," Mandy said.

"Yeah," Michelle said. "But Darla asked me to send her a video of the show. And I said yes!"

Cheeeeep! A whistle sounded throughout the playground. "Five more minutes of recess," a teacher announced.

"Oh, no." Michelle sighed again. "We can't solve this problem in only five minutes!"

"We'll think of something," Mandy told her. "Talk fast."

"Well, I'm going to audition for 'Frisco Kids' today. Aunt Becky is taking me over there after school," Michelle started to explain. "Lots of kids are trying out. I might not get the part at all. And I'm afraid Darla won't want to be my pen pal if she finds out that I'm not really on TV."

Cassie gazed at the sky. She looked as if she was thinking really hard. "I know!" she shouted.

"What?" Michelle asked.

"Are they going to videotape the try-outs?" Cassie asked.

"Yes!" Michelle smiled. She knew exactly what her friend was thinking. "I'll

45

just ask my dad to give me a copy of the videotape, right?"

"Right!" Cassie cried.

"Then it won't matter if you get the part or not," Mandy added. "You'll still have a video to send Darla."

"That's perfect!" Michelle exclaimed, hugging her two best friends.

"Ow!" Michelle yelped.

"Sorry," Aunt Becky said. "I have to get the tangles out." Becky was brushing Michelle's strawberry-blond hair. She was helping Michelle get ready for the "Frisco Kids" auditions.

Aunt Becky twisted Michelle's hair into a French braid. Then she tied it in place with a pale blue ribbon.

Michelle gazed in the big bathroom mirror behind her. "Thanks, Aunt

Becky," she said. "Now I really look like a star!"

Becky glanced at her watch. "Better hurry and get dressed," she told Michelle. "I need to get you to the studio in twenty minutes."

"Yikes!" Michelle ran to her room. Her favorite outfit was draped across the bed. She pulled on a blue striped turtleneck and black velvet overalls. She added her black high-top sneakers and she was ready.

"You look fantastic," Aunt Becky said. "Now let's get going."

Michelle and Becky hurried downstairs to the living room. The twins were playing a video game. "Come on, guys, it's time to go," Becky called.

Alex and Nicky jumped up. Michelle helped the twins slip on their jackets. Then they all piled into the car.

Michelle sat up front with Aunt Becky. Michelle was quiet; she didn't say a word. She felt butterflies in her stomach. Lots of butterflies.

"Are you nervous?" Aunt Becky asked her as they drove to the studio.

"A little," Michelle admitted. "I'm not used to being in front of a TV camera."

"Michelle's going to be on TV?" Alex asked. "I want to be on TV!"

"Me, too!" Nicky added.

Michelle giggled. "You guys are too little to be on 'Frisco Kids,' " she said.

"Not me," Alex said. "I'm big. And Daddy says if I eat my vegetables, I'll grow up to be as cool as Elvis!"

Michelle laughed. Elvis Presley was Uncle Jesse's favorite singer.

Alex began to sing an old Elvis song. The one Jesse always whistled around

48

the house. Nicky chimed in, too. Michelle sang with them. Singing with the twins made her feel a lot less nervous.

Becky pulled into the parking lot at the TV station. "Help me get these guys out of the car," she told Michelle.

Michelle was glad to have Becky, Nicky, and Alex along. Aunt Becky led her into the TV station. She helped Michelle find the makeup room. The makeup artist's name was Susie.

Susie whisked pink blush over Michelle's cheeks with a fat, soft brush. She added more blush above Michelle's eyelids.

Wow, Michelle thought. I love being a TV star!

"I think this will look great with your outfit." Susie held up a bright pink lipstick. She smoothed it on Michelle's lips. "All done!" Susie said.

An assistant stuck her head into the makeup room. "It's show time," she announced.

Michelle thanked Susie for doing her makeup. Then she followed Aunt Becky and the twins onto the "Frisco Kids" set.

The set was in a big room filled with people. Some helped set up huge bright lights. Others worked behind the television cameras.

"There's Tim Carlson. He's the 'Frisco Kids' producer." Becky pointed to a tall man holding a clipboard. He was busy giving orders to everyone.

"I forget what producers do," Michelle said.

"I guess I'm the person to ask," Becky said. "Since I'm a producer myself! It's Tim's job to find the right junior hosts. He also has to make sure everything runs smoothly today."

Tim strode up to them. "You must be Michelle," he said. He shook her hand. "You're the first one to try out. Why don't you get settled in that chair." Tim nodded toward a cushy red chair set up in front of the cameras.

Suddenly Michelle's mouth felt dry. Her stomach felt more fluttery than ever. Michelle grabbed Aunt Becky's hand. "Can all of you come to the chair with me?" she asked. "Just for a minute."

"Sure," Aunt Becky said. "But we might have to get out of the way when they start taping."

"That's okay." Michelle took her place on the chair. Her legs trembled as she sat down. She took a big, deep breath. Aunt Becky and the twins stood next to her.

"Michelle, are we on TV now?" Alex asked.

"We're like Elvis!" Nicky began to sing. Michelle giggled as the twins sang through an entire song.

Tim rushed toward them. "Stop!" he yelled, waving his hands. "Stop! Stop! Stop!"

"Oh, I'm sorry," Becky told him. "Are the twins making too much noise?"

"Too much? No, not at all!" Tim shook his head, smiling. "They were marvelous! So fresh. I loved them."

"You did?" Becky seemed surprised.

Michelle cleared her throat. "Uh, is it time to start my audition now?"

"Oh, forget the audition," Tim told her. "I just had a great idea. We'll make the show much younger. A whole new look for 'Frisco Kids'—*twin* talent! We'll use the boys as twin hosts! Don't you love it?"

"Are you serious?" Aunt Becky asked.

"Totally," Tim replied. He patted Nicky and Alex on the heads. Then he turned to the other people on the set. "Cancel the auditions," he ordered. "We've found the new stars of 'Frisco Kids'!"

Chapter

8

♥ "You didn't get the part?" Cassie turned in her seat on the bus. It was Friday. Michelle and her friends were on the way to school.

"Nope," Michelle answered. "I was just about to try out when the twins started singing. The producer loved them. He said they were the perfect hosts for 'Frisco Kids.'"

"I can't believe it!" Mandy exclaimed.

"Then you mean there's no tape for you to send to Darla?" Cassie asked.

"No," Michelle answered. "Not unless I send her a tape of Alex and Nicky singing Elvis songs."

Cassie groaned.

"I'm really sorry, Michelle," Mandy told her.

"That's okay," Michelle said. She was quiet for a moment. "Too bad I can't make my own video."

"That's a great idea, Michelle," Mandy said. "Why *don't* you make your own tape?"

"But how?" Michelle asked. "I don't have a video camera."

"Oh." Mandy looked really disappointed.

"Wait, you guys," Cassie said. "My mom has a video camera. I know how to use it. I bet she'd let me borrow it if I was really careful."

"Yeah!" Mandy slapped Michelle and Cassie each a high-five. "Another problem solved!"

"Wait a minute," Michelle said. "That won't work. The video will look totally fake. I won't be on the 'Frisco Kids' set!"

"You're right." Cassie shrugged. "I guess there's no way to solve *that* problem. We can't get into the studio."

"Nope," Mandy agreed.

Michelle stared at her friends. "Maybe we *can* get into the studio! I'll ask my dad to give us a tour. He loves to show people around the TV station."

"Great!" Cassie exclaimed. "Once we're there, we can sneak onto the set and make the video!"

"We must be the best problem solvers in the world," Mandy said.

"Yup!" Michelle grinned. "And the best friends!"

All through school, Michelle kept thinking about their secret plan. When she got home, Michelle couldn't wait to ask her dad about the studio tour.

"Michelle! Soup's on!" Danny called from the kitchen a while later.

Michelle hurried to the dinner table. She slid into her seat. Joey helped push her chair close to the table.

"Stephanie!" Danny called from the table. "Time to eat!"

"Be right there!" Stephanie yelled from upstairs.

"Hey, Dad," Michelle began. "I was telling Mandy and Cassie how neat your TV studio is. They really want to see it. Could you take us all on a special tour?"

"Could I?" A huge smile lit up Danny's face. "I'd love to, pumpkin."

"Great. Thanks, Dad," Michelle said.

"I'll show you the greenroom first," Danny went on. "That's where the stars wait before they go on the air. Then the writers' room. And, of course, the editing room, where they put the tapes together, and—"

"Wait, Danny," Joey interrupted. "You forgot an important room."

Becky frowned. "I can't think of another room."

"Room to lie down!" Joey joked. "You'll need a rest after a tour like that."

"We need a rest from your bad jokes," Jesse cracked.

Michelle laughed. "Can we do it this Saturday, Dad?"

"Okay," Danny said. "We're on for tomorrow morning."

Michelle gave her dad a huge smile. Her plan was all set.

"Michelle," Stephanie called from upstairs. "Come check the computer. You have an E-mail from Darla!"

Michelle looked at her dad. "Can I? Just for a second?"

Danny nodded. "Okay, but just for a second," he said.

Michelle bounded up the stairs to her dad's study. She pulled a chair up to the computer and read Darla's letter.

Dear Michelle,

Sorry I haven't written. I wish you could have seen me at Buckingham Palace. I wore an incredible pink satin gown. And pink roses in my hair!

I met the prince, and guess what? He kissed my hand! Next, I had tea with the queen. She was so nice. And we had the best biscuits in the world! She told me to come back anytime!

I'll be shooting in Rome for a few days! Can't wait! I'll write to you as soon as I get home.

How you are? When are you sending your video?

Michelle felt the butterflies in her stomach again. What was she going to write? What was she going to tell Darla?

Michelle took a deep breath and clicked the answer mail button.

Darla,
I'll send you my video soon.

"As soon as I can sneak into the 'Frisco Kids' studio to make it," she whispered.

Chapter

9

♥ "Hi, everybody!" Michelle said to the mirror in her room. She was practicing being a junior host for her secret "Frisco Kids" video.

Michelle flashed a giant smile. Then she frowned. "That's not right," she murmured. "I look like I'm trying too hard."

She put on a very serious expression. "Welcome to 'Frisco Kids,'" she said.

"I'm Michelle Tanner. Your junior host."

That was better. But she didn't really look like a TV host.

Her overalls and T-shirt seemed wrong.

I know! she thought. She crept over to Stephanie's closet. Stephanie's navy blue blazer hung in front of a row of clothes.

"Perfect!" Michelle pulled the jacket off the hanger and slipped it on. She checked herself out in the mirror. The jacket hung almost down to her knees!

Oh, well, she said to herself. It's *not* perfect. But it's fine for now.

She faced the mirror. "Good morning," she said in a bright, friendly voice. "I'm Michelle Tanner, the host of 'Frisco Kids'!"

Then she had a great idea.

"I'd like to say a special hello," she

told the mirror. "To my pen pal, Darla. She's a model and lives in London! Hi, Darla. Write to me soon!"

Someone burst out laughing. Michelle glanced up. "Stephanie! Don't you know how to knock?" she demanded.

"I don't have to knock to come into my own room," Stephanie shot back. She stepped through the doorway. "What are you doing, anyway?" she asked.

"Nothing," Michelle answered.

"Oh, really," Stephanie replied. "Then why are you wearing my blazer?"

Michelle yanked off the jacket and handed it to Stephanie. "I don't want it, anyway. It's too big for me."

Stephanie hung the jacket in the closet. "It sounded like you were pretending to host 'Frisco Kids,'" she said.

Michelle flopped onto her bed.

Stephanie sat beside her. "Come on, Michelle," she said. "You were, right?"

Michelle sighed. "Yes," she replied. "But it's because of my pen-pal problem."

"Problem? I thought you *liked* Darla," Stephanie said.

"I do. I like her a lot," Michelle said. "But I told her I was the star of 'Frisco Kids.' And she asked me to send her a video of me on the show! So, now I have to make one."

"Does this have something to do with touring Dad's studio?" Stephanie asked.

Michelle nodded. "Cassie and Mandy and I are going to sneak into the studio and make our own tape."

"You can't do that, Michelle," Stephanie said. "What if Dad catches you? You could get in big trouble."

"I won't," Michelle said. "Dad will never know about it."

Stephanie raised an eyebrow. "I told you not to try to impress Darla. Believe me, Michelle. You should forget about the video."

"But I can't," Michelle said. "Darla's a model! I can't let her find out I'm not a TV star. She won't want to be my pen pal anymore."

"That's silly," Stephanie said. "Friends don't care about stuff like that. Just tell Darla the truth."

"It's too late," Michelle replied. "I already promised to send her the tape."

Stephanie sighed. "Okay. But just make sure Dad doesn't find out. He'd be really angry."

Danny poked his head in the open door. "Angry?" he repeated. "What would I be angry about?"

"Uh . . . I . . . um . . ." Michelle stammered. "You'd be mad at us . . . if you caught us fighting."

Danny looked puzzled. "Were you two fighting?" he asked.

"No," Stephanie answered.

"Oh." Danny shrugged. "I'm glad." He glanced at his watch. "I've got a few things to do," he said. "I want to plan an extra-special tour for you and your friends, Michelle." He hurried down the hallway. Michelle heard him close the door to his study.

Michelle shot Stephanie a worried look. "Do you promise not to tell Dad about the tape?" she asked.

"Well, I still think you're crazy to try it," Stephanie told her. "But, okay. I promise."

"Thanks." Michelle grinned. "Don't worry, Stephanie. We've got the perfect plan. Dad will never find out."

Chapter

10

♥ "Everybody line up!" Danny announced Saturday morning. "The next stop on our private studio tour is the greenroom!"

Michelle, Cassie, and Mandy followed Danny down a long hallway.

"It's getting late, Michelle," Cassie whispered. "When are we going to make your tape?"

"I don't know," Michelle whispered

back. "We have to wait for a chance to be alone."

Danny stopped in front of a closed wooden door. "This is the greenroom," he announced as he opened it. "Where the guests wait before they go on the show." They stepped inside the room.

Michelle noticed the peach-colored walls and the cozy blue sofas and chairs. She wrinkled her nose. "But there's nothing *green* in this room!" she said.

Danny laughed. "I know. Every TV station and theater calls their waiting area the greenroom. Nobody really knows why."

Mandy poked Michelle. "I hope the 'Frisco Kids' studio is our next stop," she whispered.

"It must be," Michelle replied.

"Our next stop is the video library," Danny announced. "You'll find it very interesting," he explained. "It's filled with tapes instead of books."

"Yeah. Interesting," Cassie muttered.

Michelle and her friends followed Danny down another hall. They passed the ladies' room. Then they passed a door that had a red lightbulb over it.

"That's the studio," Danny told them. "We'll see it last."

"Wait, Dad!" Michelle exchanged looks with Mandy and Cassie. Now was the perfect chance to make their secret video. "Um, we have to go to the bathroom."

"Okay, girls," Danny said. "I'll wait for you here."

"No!" Mandy blurted out. "Uh . . . I mean . . ."

"Danny!" A dark-haired man called out. He waved his arms. "I'm glad

69

you're here. Could I talk to you in my office for a minute? I need your help."

Danny looked at the girls. "I'll meet you in the video library in five minutes," he said. "It's just down the hall. Can you find your way?"

"No problem," Michelle answered. "See you soon."

"Okay, Bob," he said to the man. "Let's go."

Michelle and her friends hurried into the ladies' room. Michelle peeked out a minute later. Her father was gone.

"That was lucky!" she exclaimed. "Cassie, you and I will sneak into the studio. Mandy, you stay outside and make sure no one catches us."

Mandy nodded. "Okay."

"Wait a minute," Michelle told her. "We need a password. A way to warn us if someone's coming." She thought for a second. "How about *action*?"

"Sounds good," Mandy said.

Michelle pulled open the door to the studio. Mandy waited in the hallway, while Michelle and Cassie slipped inside.

A few chairs were lined up at the front of the room. TV cameras stood against one wall.

"I'll sit in that chair." Michelle pointed to the big red one in the middle of the set.

Cassie pulled her mother's video camera out of her backpack. She placed it over an eye and pushed a button. "Oh, no," Cassie groaned. "I can't get it to work!"

"Let me see it," Michelle said, hopping off the chair. "Maybe I can figure it out."

"The light isn't on," Mandy said. "That means it's not working. Now we won't be able to make the video!"

Michelle looked at the camera. Then she flicked the on/off switch. A little red light came on. Michelle giggled. "You forgot to turn it on, silly!"

"Oops!" Cassie said.

Michelle took her place on the cushy chair. This is great, she thought. I think I'll send Darla the video tonight.

Cassie held the camera up to one eye. "Rolling!" she said.

Michelle flashed her best junior-anchor smile. "Good morning, everyone! I'm your host, Michelle Tanner." Then she looked directly into the camera. "You're going to love today's episode of 'Frisco Kids'! We're going to—"

Bang! Michelle heard the studio door slam open.

Mandy burst into the room, waving her arms in the air. "Action! Action! Action!"

Chapter

11

♥ "Your dad is coming," Mandy cried. "Hide!"

A second later Danny appeared in the doorway. "I thought you girls were going to the bathroom," he said.

"We did," Michelle said quickly. "Uh, then we got lost."

"I see," Danny said. "Well, this time I'll take you myself. But we're running out of time, so let's hurry."

Michelle gave Cassie and Mandy a

worried look. They had to follow Danny back to the video library.

He showed them row after row of shelves stacked with videotapes.

"Really nice," Michelle told him.

"And very neat," Danny said. He ran his finger along a desktop and held it up. "See, no dust! Next stop is the editing room. They keep it neat and clean, too," he said.

Michelle shook her head. Dad is just as picky about cleaning at work as he is at home, Michelle thought.

They stepped into the hallway.

"Hold it, Dad," Michelle told him. "Um, I think I dropped my scrunchie back in the bathroom. I have to go back and get it."

"Aren't you interested in the rest of the tour, Michelle?" Danny asked.

"You're the one who wanted to do this."

"Sure, I'm interested," Michelle said. "But that was my favorite scrunchie. I have to find it!"

"All right," Danny said. "I'll take you back to the bathroom so you don't get lost again."

"No!" Michelle cried. "I mean, you don't have to. We know the way. Really."

Michelle, Mandy, and Cassie hurried toward the bathroom again. Then, when they were sure no one was watching, they ran back into the studio. Mandy stayed by the door.

Cassie quickly pulled her video camera from her backpack. "You're on!" she told Michelle. "Hurry!"

Michelle smiled. "Hi, I'm Michelle

Tanner! And you're watching 'Frisco Kids.' "

"Oh, no! Action!" Mandy cried from the door. She dashed to the back of the room. "Someone's coming!"

"What do we do?" Cassie yelled. "What do we do?"

Michelle spotted a closet door. "Quick," she said, and flung the door open. "Let's hide in here!"

Michelle, Mandy, and Cassie piled in. Michelle pulled the door shut.

The closet was crammed full of mops, brooms, and a very stinky bucket.

"Yuck! This is gross," Cassie said.

"Someone's poking me," Mandy complained. "This closet is too small,"

"We'll only be in here for a minute," Michelle whispered. She listened carefully at the door.

"Do you hear anything?" Mandy asked.

"Nope, I think they're gone," she said. Then Michelle reached for the door-knob. She turned it back and forth, but it wouldn't budge.

"Oh, no!" Michelle cried. "We're locked in!"

Chapter
12

♥ "No!" Cassie yelled. "We can't be locked in!" She pushed her way to the front of the closet and banged her fists on the door. "Helllp!"

Mandy pounded on the door, too. "Get us out of here!"

Click.

The doorknob turned, and the door swung open.

Michelle, Cassie, and Mandy tumbled out of the closet—right into Danny.

Michelle looked at her father. "Uh, hi, Dad."

Danny stared down at them. He looked puzzled when he saw Cassie holding her video camera. "Michelle, what is going on?" he asked.

"Would you believe we're looking for my scrunchie?" Michelle smiled weakly.

Danny shook his head. "I think you'd better tell me the real story," he said.

Michelle took a deep breath. "It all started with my pen pal, Darla," she began. "She's just so cool!"

"That's why you sneaked into the studio?" Danny asked. "Because your pen pal is cool?"

"Not exactly," Michelle said. "I wanted to be as interesting as Darla . . . so I told her I was the host of 'Frisco Kids.' And then I didn't get the part.

And then she asked me for a tape of the show. And—"

"I think I see it now," Danny said. "You came in here to make a phony tape."

Michelle hung her head. "I'm sorry, Dad."

"Well, Michelle, I hope you'll learn something from this," Danny said.

"About telling the truth?" Michelle asked.

"Yes. Telling the truth is always best," her dad answered. "But there's something else that's just as important."

"What else?" Michelle asked.

"Being yourself," Danny answered. "People have to like the real you," he said. "Or else they can never be your real friend. You have to give Darla a chance to know the real you. So she can *like* the real you."

"That's just what Stephanie told me!" Michelle exclaimed.

"Do you believe that now, Michelle?" Danny asked. "Not being yourself almost always gets you in trouble."

"No kidding," Michelle replied. "I'm going to tell Darla the truth—tonight!"

Danny smiled. "That makes me proud of you," he said. "You're the best kid, ever."

"And you're the best *dad,* ever," Michelle told him.

"Are you trying to talk your way to Ice Cream City?" Danny joked.

"Yay!" Cassie and Mandy cried. "You're the greatest, Mr. Tanner."

"I thought you guys liked me for myself," Danny teased.

"We do," Michelle answered. "Almost as much as we like chocolate sprinkles!"

Danny grinned at Michelle. "Now you are *definitely* acting like yourself."

Dear Darla,
There's something I have to tell you. This is really hard for me to say. But I have to say it.

"Oops!" Michelle punched the send key before she was done. A minute later a message appeared on the computer screen: YOU'VE GOT MAIL! Michelle stared as a letter appeared across the screen:

Hi, Michelle!
I can't believe you were writing to me at the same time I was writing to you! What do you have to tell me?
Darla

Michelle took a deep breath and typed a reply:

I want to say I'm sorry for lying to you. The truth is, I'm not the host of "Frisco Kids." I'm not even on TV. I never was.

The screen was blank for a long time. Oh, no! Michelle thought. Darla doesn't want to be my pen pal anymore! She typed another message:

Darla,
Are you still there? Are you mad at me?

Finally, Darla typed back:

Hi, Michelle,
I'm still here.
And I have something to tell you, too.

Michelle felt really nervous. What if Darla told her to get lost—for good?

I don't care if you're on TV or not! Besides, I'm not really a model! That wasn't even me in the picture from the magazine.

After you told me your dad and your aunt were on TV, I thought I had to make up something exciting about me. I was afraid you'd think my life was boring.

I hope you're not mad, Michelle. I'm sorry I made up all that stuff about working in Rome and Paris. Will you forgive me?

                                        Darla

Michelle couldn't believe it. All this time, Darla was trying to be someone else, too!

Michelle laughed out loud as she typed her reply:

Dear Darla,

Definitely! I think you're cool just for being you! And the best thing is, we don't have to pretend anymore! Let's promise to always be friends, and never tell any more lies. And don't cross your fingers when you type back!

Darla typed a short reply:

You're funny, Michelle! I promise— without crossing my fingers!

Oops! My dad just yelled for me to wash the dinner dishes. I forgot. That's what my real life is like! Will you write me again tomorrow?

Darla

"Michelle!" Stephanie yelled up the stairs. "It's your turn to do the lunch dishes!"

"Just a minute!" Michelle called back. She turned to the computer again.

Dear Darla,

My sister just yelled for me to wash the dishes, too! I guess we're a lot alike after all. And I promise I'll write back tomorrow. As myself!

Love, Michelle

FULL HOUSE™

SISTERS

A brand-new series starring Stephanie AND Michelle!

#1 Two On The Town

Stephanie and Michelle find themselves
in the big city—and in big trouble!

(Coming in mid-November 1998)

#2 One Boss Too Many

Stephanie and Michelle think camp will be major fun.
If only these two sisters were getting along!

(Coming in mid-December 1998)

When sisters get together...expect the unexpected!

A MINSTREL® BOOK

Published by Pocket Books

2012

It doesn't matter if you live around the corner...
or around the world...
If you are a fan of Mary-Kate and Ashley Olsen,
you should be a member of

MARY-KATE + ASHLEY'S FUN CLUB™

Here's what you get:
Our Funzine™
An autographed color photo
Two black & white individual photos
A full size color poster
An official **Fun Club**™ membership card
A **Fun Club**™ school folder
Two special **Fun Club**™ surprises
A holiday card
Fun Club™ collectibles catalog
Plus a **Fun Club**™ box to keep everything in

To join Mary-Kate + Ashley's Fun Club™, fill out the form
below and send it along with

U.S. Residents – $17.00
Canadian Residents – $22 U.S. Funds
International Residents – $27 U.S. Funds

MARY-KATE + ASHLEY'S FUN CLUB™
859 HOLLYWOOD WAY, SUITE 275
BURBANK, CA 91505

NAME:_____

ADDRESS:_____

_CITY:_____ STATE:_____ ZIP:_____

PHONE:(____) _____ BIRTHDATE:_____

1242

FULL HOUSE Stephanie™

PHONE CALL FROM A FLAMINGO	88004-7/$3.99
THE BOY-OH-BOY NEXT DOOR	88121-3/$3.99
TWIN TROUBLES	88290-2/$3.99
HIP HOP TILL YOU DROP	88291-0/$3.99
HERE COMES THE BRAND NEW ME	89858-2/$3.99
THE SECRET'S OUT	89859-0/$3.99
DADDY'S NOT-SO-LITTLE GIRL	89860-4/$3.99
P.S. FRIENDS FOREVER	89861-2/$3.99
GETTING EVEN WITH THE FLAMINGOES	52273-6/$3.99
THE DUDE OF MY DREAMS	52274-4/$3.99
BACK-TO-SCHOOL COOL	52275-2/$3.99
PICTURE ME FAMOUS	52276-0/$3.99
TWO-FOR-ONE CHRISTMAS FUN	53546-3/$3.99
THE BIG FIX-UP MIX-UP	53547-1/$3.99
TEN WAYS TO WRECK A DATE	53548-X/$3.99
WISH UPON A VCR	53549-8/$3.99
DOUBLES OR NOTHING	56841-8/$3.99
SUGAR AND SPICE ADVICE	56842-6/$3.99
NEVER TRUST A FLAMINGO	56843-4/$3.99
THE TRUTH ABOUT BOYS	00361-5/$3.99
CRAZY ABOUT THE FUTURE	00362-3/$3.99
MY SECRET ADMIRER	00363-1/$3.99
BLUE RIBBON CHRISTMAS	00830-7/$3.99
THE STORY ON OLDER BOYS	00831-5/$3.99
MY THREE WEEKS AS A SPY	00832-3/$3.99
NO BUSINESS LIKE SHOW BUSINESS	01725-X/$3.99

 Available from Minstrel® Books Published by Pocket Books

Simon & Schuster Mail Order Dept. BWB
200 Old Tappan Rd., Old Tappan, N.J. 07675

Please send me the books I have checked above. I am enclosing $_____(please add $0.75 to cover the postage and handling for each order. Please add appropriate sales tax). Send check or money order--no cash or C.O.D.'s please. Allow up to six weeks for delivery. For purchase over $10.00 you may use VISA: card number, expiration date and customer signature must be included.

Name _____

Address _____

City _____ State/Zip _____

VISA Card # _____ Exp.Date _____

Signature _____

929-23